THE WIND IN THE WILLOWS

by KENNETH GRAHAME

#5 Sneaky Toad

Adapted by Laura Driscoll

Illustrated by Ann Iosa

STERLING

New York / London

www.sterlingpublishing.com/kids

STERLING and the distinctive Sterling logo are registered trademarks
of Sterling Publishing Co., Inc.

Library of Congress Cataloging-in-Publication Data Available

Lot #: 02/10
10 9 8 7 6 5 4 3 2 1

Published by Sterling Publishing Co., Inc.
387 Park Avenue South, New York, NY 10016
© 2010 by Sterling Publishing Co., Inc.
Illustrations © 2010 by Ann Iosa
Distributed in Canada by Sterling Publishing
c/o Canadian Manda Group, 165 Dufferin Street
Toronto, Ontario, Canada M6K 3H6
Distributed in the United Kingdom by GMC Distribution Services
Castle Place, 166 High Street, Lewes, East Sussex, England BN7 1XU
Distributed in Australia by Capricorn Link (Australia) Pty. Ltd.
P.O. Box 704, Windsor, NSW 2756, Australia

Printed in China
All rights reserved

Sterling ISBN 978 1-4027-6729-6

For information about custom editions, special sales, premium and
corporate purchases, please contact Sterling Special Sales
Department at 800-805-5489 or specialsales@sterlingpublishing.com.

Contents

Bad Toad

Bad Toad

Mole, Rat, and Badger
were worried about Toad.
Toad had lots of money.
He had bought lots of
new cars with his money.
The problem was that Toad
could not drive very well.
He had wrecked
all of his nice new cars!

Badger tried to talk to Toad.
"You must not drive until
you learn how," Badger said.
"Try to be more careful, Toad!"
"You are right," said Toad.
"From now on,
I will be more careful."

Badger, Rat, and Mole
knew Toad very well.
They knew Toad did not always do
what he said he would do.
They thought he might need help
being a careful Toad.

So they made a plan.

Rat and Mole went home,

but Badger stayed at Toad's house.

He wanted to keep an eye on Toad.

Toad was not sure
he liked that plan!
"This is my house," said Toad,
"and those cars are my cars.
I can drive them if I want to!"

Deep down,
Toad did not want
to be a careful Toad.

So sneaky Toad hopped out
the window and he ran away—
away from his home
and away from his friends.

The Car

"Ha, ha!" Toad said.
"What a clever Toad I am!"
He was on his own.
No one could tell him
what he should do
or what he should not do.

Toad walked along a road.

He heard a noise.

Beep-beep! Beep-beep!

A car was coming toward him.

"Oooo!" said Toad.

"What a lovely, shiny red car."

Toad waved.

The car stopped.

Inside were two bears.

"Excuse me, sirs," Toad said.

"I have walked a long way.

I am very tired.

Are you headed to town?"

"Yes," said the driver.
"Would you like a ride?"
"Yes, please," said Toad—
but that was not the whole truth.
Toad did not just want
to *ride* in the car.
Toad wanted to *drive* the car.

Splash!

The bears helped Toad
into the back seat,
and off they went.
They drove a few miles.
Then sneaky Toad said,
"Thank you for the ride,
but . . . may I sit up front?
I need some fresh air."

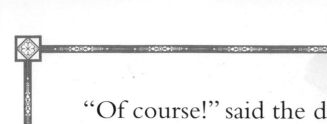

"Of course!" said the driver.

He stopped the car.

The other bear got into the back seat.

Toad got into the front seat.

Then off they went.

They drove a few more miles.

Then Toad said, "May I try to drive?

It looks so easy and fun!"

The driver laughed.
"Well, okay." he said.
"I will let you try."

So the driver stopped the car.

He got into the back seat.

Toad got into the driver's seat.

At first, Toad drove slowly.

The two bears clapped.

"Well done!" said the driver.

Then Toad drove faster and faster!

"Be careful!" said the driver.

But Toad did not want to be
a careful Toad!

So Toad drove on.

He swerved to the left.

He swerved to the right.

Splash!

The car went off the road,

through a bush, and into a pond.

Toad had wrecked *another* car!

The End?

Toad got up and ran away.

"Ha, ha!" he said.

"What a clever Toad I am!"

Then Toad saw that

he had spoken too soon.

When he looked back,

the bears were after him!

"Oh, my!" he said.

"If only I had learned to drive,

I would not be in this mess.

From now on,

I *will* be a careful Toad."

Then Toad looked up.
Just ahead, he saw a hole
in the riverbank.
The fast water carried Toad
toward the hole.

Toad reached up.
He grabbed on to
the edge of the hole.
He pulled himself up
and out of the water.

He huffed. He puffed.

He peered inside the hole.

Do you know what he saw?

He saw Rat!

Toad had washed up

at Rat's house.

He was safe!

"Rat!" said Toad.

"I have learned my lesson.

From now on,

I *will* be a careful Toad."

Rat hoped it was true.

Because if there was

one thing he knew…

. . . it was that Toad did not always
do what he said he would do.